CONTENTS

ACTIVITY PAGES

STORIES BY IAN ROBINSON

ILLUSTRATED BY JOHN HARROLD

STORY COLOURING BY DORIS CAMPBELL AND GINA HART

John Harrold.

RUPERT

THE DAILY EXPRESS ANNUAL

John Harrold.

Pedigree
BOOKS

No 58

Published by Pedigree Books Limited
The Old Rectory, Matford Lane, Exeter, Devon, EX2 4PS.

RUPERT

*"Look, Bill!" cries Rupert. "See how my
New model aeroplane will fly . . ."*

It is a sunny autumn morning and Rupert and
Bill have gone to Nutwood common to fly
Rupert's new model glider. "Hurrah!" cries Bill as
Rupert launches the plane. "It flies really well!"
Rupert smiles as he watches it glide smoothly
through the air. "Not bad for a first flight!" he
chuckles. "Your turn to try next, Bill." As he
speaks, a tremendous wind suddenly starts to blow
and carries the glider up, high above the pals' heads.

and Ottoline

*Success! But as they watch it go
A sudden strong wind starts to blow.*

*The pals give chase as fast as they
Can run. It mustn't get away!*

"Quick, Bill!" calls Rupert, hurrying after the glider. "We mustn't let it out of our sight!" The two chums race across the common and are just in time to see the plane heading off over the trees. Too intent on the glider to notice where they are going, the pair keep running until they come to a high wall which rings a private garden. "Oh, no!" groans Bill, as the plane flies over the wall. "Anywhere but there . . ."

*They're just in time to see it fall
Behind a crumbling garden wall . . .*

RUPERT CLIMBS THE WALL

"Old Nutwood Manor!" Rupert cries.
"They say it's haunted!" Bill replies.

"Ghosts?" Rupert scoffs. "There's no such thing!
Just help me up – stop worrying!"

"Hurrah!" calls Rupert. "I can see
The plane. It's in an apple tree . . ."

He runs to fetch it, but can hear
A groaning sound from somewhere near!

Rupert's glider has landed in the garden of a deserted old house called Nutwood Manor. "What's so terrible about that?" he asks Bill. "We can easily clamber over the wall . . ." "It's haunted!" says Bill. "Nonsense!" declares Rupert. "It's just an empty house. Even if there *are* any ghosts, I'm sure they only come out at night." As Rupert is so determined to look for his plane, Bill agrees to help him. "Be careful," he warns. "Come back as soon as you find it!"

From the top of the wall Rupert can see an overgrown orchard and a glimpse of Nutwood Manor in the distance. "There's the glider!" he cries. "I can see it, stuck in the branches of one of the trees . . ." Climbing down, he makes his way over towards the tree. He hasn't gone far when he suddenly hears a low groaning sound. "Crikey!" gasps Rupert, stopping in his tracks. "Perhaps Bill was right and Nutwood Manor *is* haunted after all!"

RUPERT DISCOVERS PODGY

It's not a ghost that Rupert's found –
For Podgy made the groaning sound . . .

He climbed the apple tree to scrump
Then ate too much, the greedy chump!

"Who's there?" calls Bill, then blinks to see
His portly pal climb down the tree.

The chums are ready to depart
When something makes them turn and start!

Telling himself not to be frightened, Rupert tip-toes forward and reaches up for the glider. There is a rustle of leaves and the next moment he sees a familiar face peering down through the branches. "Podgy!" he cries. "Sorry if I startled you," says Podgy. "I climbed up to pick some apples. As the old house is empty it seems a shame to let them go to waste . . ." "Why were you making that terrible noise?" asks Rupert. "I've eaten too many," groans Podgy.

As Podgy starts to climb down, Bill's head appears above the top of the wall. "Is everything all right?" he calls. "Who was that I could hear you talking to?" "Only Podgy!" laughs Rupert and explains how he caught their chum scrumping apples. "I'm glad I managed to find the glider," he says. "Podgy can come and join us for a second flight." He is about to hand the plane up to Bill when the pals are shocked to hear the sound of an approaching lorry . . .

9

RUPERT SEES SOMEONE ARRIVE

A lorry suddenly appears –
The first time one's been here for years!

"Removal men!" gasps Rupert. "Then
There's someone living here again!"

A car arrives as Rupert goes –
It isn't anyone he knows . . .

The whole thing's quite a mystery,
Whoever can the owner be?

The startled pals look towards the house and are amazed to see a large van pulling up outside. "What's happening?" asks Podgy. "Nobody's lived here for years . . ." Two men get out of the lorry and unfold the tail-gate. "They're unloading furniture," whispers Rupert. "You're right," says Podgy as the men carry a huge piano out of the van. "It looks as though someone must be moving in to Nutwood Manor. I wonder who it can be?"

As Rupert and Podgy watch the men unload more furniture, they are alarmed to hear a car turn in at the main gate and come racing up the drive. "Come on!" hisses Rupert. "Let's get back before we're spotted!" "Who was it?" asks Bill when he hears about the car. "I couldn't see," replies Podgy. "They were too far away." "Never mind," says Rupert. "I expect we'll find out soon enough. Let's go and fly the glider again."

END OF PART 1

How carefully can you colour these two pictures of Rupert?

PART 2

RUPERT
and Ottoline

Next day, at school, the chums all hear
A new girl's come to join their year . . .

When Ottoline arrives they see
Whose home the Manor House must be!

A music lesson starts the day –
"You sing," says Dr. Chimp. "I'll play . . ."

But Dr. Chimp can't play for long,
"My goodness, all this music's wrong!"

The next day, when Rupert and his pals arrive for school, they are surprised to hear Dr. Chimp announce that there will be a new pupil joining their class. "She's called Ottoline," he explains. "Her family have just moved to Nutwood." Before Dr. Chimp can say any more, a big car pulls up at the school gates and a mother otter comes hurrying in with her daughter. "It's the same car we saw yesterday!" gasps Podgy.

As soon as Ottoline has been introduced to the class, Dr. Chimp begins a music lesson. "It's time we started practising for the school concert!" he declares. "I'll begin with an easy song so you can all join in." Opening the lid of the piano, Dr. Chimp settles down in front of his music and begins to play. "Goodness me!" he gasps as he turns the page. "This isn't the same piece at all!" As he peers at the music the Fox brothers start to giggle . . .

RUPERT MAKES A NEW FRIEND

The naughty Fox twins laugh with glee –
They've mixed it up deliberately!

"Please sir," cries Ottoline. "I know
exactly how that tune should go!"

"I've always played!" she tells the chums
When finally the lunch-break comes.

"You spoiled our fun!" glares Freddy. "Now
We'll play a joke on you somehow . . ."

What can have happened to Dr. Chimp's music? Rupert notices the Fox brothers laughing to themselves. "Of course!" he thinks. "They must have muddled everything up while he was out of the room." "Please sir," says Ottoline, "I know that tune. I can play it for you . . ." To everyone's astonishment she sits down at the piano and starts to play the piece – without any music at all! "Bravo!" beams Dr. Chimp. "I think *you* should play in the school concert!"

When the morning's lessons end and everyone goes for lunch, Rupert and Bill ask Ottoline how she learnt to play the piano so well. "It's easy when you practice as much as I do," she smiles. "I started having lessons when I was very young." As they talk, Rupert spots the Fox brothers coming into the dining room. "Aren't you going to join us?" he asks. "No!" says Freddy. "We're not having lunch with *her*. She spoilt our joke with Dr. Chimp's music!"

*Later that week, Rupert finds he
Is asked to Ottoline's for tea . . .*

*He meets Bill as he's on the way,
"We'll see* inside *the house today!"*

*"Hello!" calls Ottoline. "Come in!
I'll show you round, then we'll begin . . ."*

*"It's still so cluttered! No-one knows
Where any of these objects goes!"*

A few days later, the postman calls at the Bears' house with a letter addressed to Rupert. "Who is it from?" asks Mrs. Bear. "Ottoline!" smiles Rupert. "She's having a party this afternoon and wants to know if I can come." "Of course," says Mrs. Bear. "Why don't you take her a nice bunch of flowers?" On the way to Nutwood Manor, Rupert meets Bill Badger, who has also been invited. "I can't wait to see inside," he declares. "I wonder what it's like?"

The two pals make their way up the long drive to the house and Rupert tugs at the bell-pull. "Hello!" cries Ottoline as she opens the door. "I'm so glad that you could both come." Thanking them for their gifts, she leads the way inside, past a clutter of packing chests and dust-sheets. "There's still a lot to do," explains Ottoline. "The house has been standing empty for so long that nobody can remember what's here, or where it should go!"

"Who's that?" asks Bill. "An otter who
Once lived in Nutwood Manor too . . ."

The doorbell rings and inside comes
The rest of Ottoline's new chums.

A splendid feast with treats in store –
But what's that moaning sound next door?

"A g..g..g..g..ghost!" cries Bill.
It seems the Manor's haunted still . . .

As they walk further into the house, Bill spots a huge portrait of an otter, dressed in old-fashioned clothes. "That's one of my ancestors!" laughs Ottoline. "He used to own Nutwood Manor, but was forced to give it up during the Civil War. When my father heard the house was for sale, he couldn't resist buying it and moving back to Nutwood." The doorbell rings as more of the chums arrive. "Come in," smiles Ottoline. "Now we're all here, let's go and have some tea . . ."

Ottoline's party is a splendid affair, held in the panelled dining room of the old house. Mrs. Otter brings in cakes, jellies, sandwiches and a large jug of lemonade, which she has just started to pour when there is a low moan from the next room. "What's that?" gulps Bill. Rupert opens the door and peers out cautiously. At first he can see nothing but, as the others arrive, a strange white figure appears on the stairs. "It's a ghost!" gasps Bill.

PART 3

RUPERT
and Ottoline

Two ghosts come floating down the stairs.
"I didn't know they came in pairs!"

Then, as the pals look on in fear,
They see the first ghost disappear!

"What's happening?" the second calls,
Then stumbles on the stairs and falls . . .

"Look!" Rupert cries. "It's all a hoax!
Another of the Foxes' jokes!"

"I knew Nutwood Manor was haunted!" cries Bill as the ghost advances slowly down the stairs, followed by a second shadowy form. Rupert shakes his head in disbelief. "I didn't know ghosts came in pairs," he whispers to Ottoline. Suddenly, the second ghost seems to stumble and clutches wildly at the banister to try to prevent himself falling. To the pals astonishment, a trapdoor swings open below the first ghost, who tumbles through it with a wail of dismay . . .

No sooner has the first ghost vanished than the trap-door swings back with a click. "What's happened, Freddy?" cries the second ghost, stumbling downstairs until he lands in a sprawling heap. "I thought so!" cries Rupert, as a hand reaches out from beneath a large white sheet. "It's Ferdy Fox!" gasps Edward as Rupert lifts the sheet to reveal the shame-faced hoaxer underneath. "It was only a joke," he quavers. "We didn't mean to spoil the party . . .

RUPERT AND OTTOLINE VANISH

Ottoline laughs, "You fooled us all!
But where did your poor brother fall?"

As Edward tugs the stair-post he
reveals a trapdoor suddenly!

Rupert and Ottoline fall through
The secret door and vanish too . . .

"A tunnel!" Rupert cries, but then
The ghostly groaning starts again!

"Never mind," smiles Ottoline. "This is the most exciting party I've ever had! The important thing now is to rescue your brother . . ." "I still don't know what happened," says Ferdy. "We were coming downstairs together, when I tripped and fell against the banister. That seemed to open the trapdoor." "Perhaps if I give it a tug?" suggests Edward. There is a loud click and the trapdoor opens again, plunging Rupert and Ottoline down through the floor . . .

As the trapdoor snaps shut above them, Rupert and Ottoline land with a bump at the bottom of a steep-sided pit. "Are you all right?" asks Rupert helping Ottoline to her feet. "Yes, thanks," she says. "Just a bit startled!" "There's a tunnel!" cries Rupert. "Let's see where it leads." The pair set off towards the light, but as they enter the tunnel they are stopped in their tracks by a groaning sound which echoes in the darkness. "More ghosts!" shudders Ottoline.

It's Freddy Fox! He's here as well,
But hurt his ankle when he fell . . .

"Come on!" says Ottoline. "If we
Both help he'll be all right, you'll see!"

At last they reach a secret door.
"That must be the way out, I'm sure . . ."

It opens stiffly, with a creak,
But what's there? Rupert takes a peek . . .

Despite the strange moans they can hear, Rupert and Ottoline decide to keep going, in the hope of finding a way out. As they turn a corner, they see Freddy Fox, sitting on the ground. "So, it was you we could hear," says Rupert. "That's right," groans Freddy. "I hurt my ankle." "Never mind," says Ottoline. "Rupert and I will help you to the end of the tunnel." "Thanks," says Freddy as he hobbles along. "I'm sorry our joke caused so much fuss . . ."

As the three chums reach the end of the tunnel they see a heavy wooden door with two small holes in it. "How odd!" exclaims Ottoline. "It's almost as if we were inside a secret room . . ." "I wish it had some chairs in it," groans Freddy. "Rest on this old box while I see if the door will open," says Rupert. He pulls on the handle which turns stiffly, as though nobody has used it for a long time. The door swings open and he peers round it to see what's on the other side.

RUPERT'S PAL DISCOVERS A CHEST

"Your ancestor!" laughs Rupert. "He
Kept the door hidden – come and see!"

"We found a way out!" Rupert cries.
"Thank goodness!" Mrs. Otter sighs.

Then Freddy Fox announces he
Has made a great discovery!

An ancient chest! The pals decide
They'll take a closer look outside . . .

"W . . . where are we?" asks Ottoline as she steps through the doorway. "Come and see!" laughs Rupert. "It's the painting of your old ancestor!" "How extraordinary," cries Ottoline. "We're back in the main hall!" "I wonder if the others are still looking for us?" asks Rupert. He hurries to the staircase and, sure enough, the chums are all gathered around, trying to make the trapdoor open. "Thank goodness you're both safe!" cries Mrs. Otter.

When Rupert explains how he and Ottoline escaped, everyone hurries to see the secret door. "Fancy that!" gasps Mrs. Otter. "This house is full of surprises." "Freddy Fox is here too," says Ottoline, helping him into the hall. "I've made a discovery!" says Freddy excitedly. "That box I was sitting on looks like some sort of chest." Rupert peers at the dusty box. "It *is* a chest!" he cries. "Come on, Edward, help Podgy and me to carry it into the light."

RUPERT FINDS OUT WHAT'S INSIDE

As Ottoline dusts off the chest
She finds a coat of arms, "Our Crest!"

The rusty lock undoes and she
Lifts up the lid excitedly . . .

"There's something here I recognise!
My ancestor's old clothes!" she cries.

The only treasure is a purse
of pennies – still it could be worse!

Curious to see what it looks like, everyone gathers round the ancient chest. "It's terribly dusty," says Bill. "I don't suppose anyone has moved it for ages . . ." Rupert rubs at the grimy lid and is amazed to uncover an elaborate coat of arms. "It's the same as my ancestor's!" cries Ottoline. "Just like the portrait." At first the chest seems firmly locked, but by pulling together at the rusty catches, Rupert and Ottoline finally manage to prise open the lid and peer inside . . .

"Is it full of treasure?" asks Freddy. "Not exactly . . ." says Ottoline, as she lifts out a wide-brimmed hat. "It seems to be full of my ancestor's clothes!" "They're the same as he's wearing in the portrait," laughs Rupert. Reaching inside the chest, Rupert comes across a leather purse which chinks as he picks it up. "You've found treasure after all," smiles Mrs. Otter, when he shows her the coins. "They're Civil War pennies, from the time of King Charles . . ."

RUPERT HAS A SPECIAL PRESENT

*"Tea-time!" says Ottoline. "Now you
Fox twins must join my party too . . ."*

*And after tea, the whole group plays
In fancy dress from olden days . . .*

*Then all the pals thank Ottoline
For the best party that there's been!*

*"What's that you've got?" asks Rupert's Mum.
"A special present from my chum!"*

"Now that everyone's safe and sound, let's have tea," suggests Ottoline's mother. "You must be hungry after all that excitement." "Can we come too?" asks Freddy. "Of course," says Ottoline, taking the brothers by the arm. "I know you didn't mean any harm by your joke. Let's be friends . . ." After they have finished tea, the pals go out into the garden to play with the chest full of old clothes. "What fun!" laughs Ottoline. "A fancy dress party!"

At last, when it's time to go home, everyone agrees that Ottoline's party has been the best they've ever had. "Thanks for coming!" she calls as Bill and Rupert wave goodbye. "See you at school tomorrow." "I'm glad it ended so happily," says Mrs. Bear when Rupert tells her all about the "ghost". "Look what Ottoline gave me," he smiles. "A coin from her ancestor's purse, as a souvenir!"

THE END

RUPERT and

Rupert goes shopping with a list.
"Stamps!" cries his Mum. "That's what I've missed!"

One day, Rupert's mother asks him to go and do some shopping. "I think that's all," she says as she hands him a list. "Oh, yes, there's something I've forgotten. Please ask for half a dozen stamps. We've run out and I want to write some letters." Rupert promises to remember and sets out towards the shops. He hasn't gone far when he spots his friend, Pong-Ping. "Wait for me!" he calls and hurries to catch up.

the Chinese Creeper

As Rupert nears the High Street he
Spots Pong-Ping and calls, "Wait for me!"

Pong-Ping has got to buy stamps too.
"I'll come and get them now, with you . . ."

"Hello, Rupert!" says Pong-Ping. "I'm going to
the shops too. I want to buy some stamps to
send a letter to China. I've got to write and thank
my uncle for a present he's just sent me . . ."
"What is it?" asks Rupert. "A box!" his chum
replies as they reach the shop. "Actually, it's
rather mysterious. Why don't you come to my
house and have a look? I'd like to know what you
think . . ."

His uncle's sent a gift which he
Would like Rupert to come and see . . .

RUPERT OPENS A STRANGE BOX

*Pong-Ping's old uncle often sends
Strange gifts that mystify his friends . . .*

*"A puzzle box!" says Pong-Ping. "I
Can't open it – you have a try!"*

*"In China they are used to hide
Some precious gift that's locked inside . . ."*

*Rupert tries to undo the box,
It twists and suddenly unlocks!*

As soon as Rupert has filled his basket and the two pals have bought their stamps, they set off for Pong-Ping's house. "My uncle often sends me strange presents from China," declares Pong-Ping as they walk along, "but this is the strangest yet!" When they reach his house he leads the way into the sitting room and points to a small painted box that's lying on the table. "There it is," he chuckles. "Let's see if you have any more luck in getting it to open than I did . . ."

Rupert picks up the box and examines it closely. "I can't see how it opens at all!" he tells Pong-Ping. "There isn't any sign of a lid." "Exactly!" laughs the peke. "It's a puzzle box. Most of them have some sort of hidden catch, but this one seems impossible . . ." At that moment, Rupert gives the box a twist and feels the top half slowly start to turn. "Look!" he cries. "The petals of the flower are unfolding." "So *that's* how it works . . ." gasps Pong-Ping.

RUPERT SEES WHAT'S INSIDE

"Look, Rupert!" Pong-Ping gives a shout –
As two small envelopes fall out . . .

"A note from Uncle!" cries Pong-Ping.
"In which he explains everything . . ."

"He's sent some Chinese Creeper seeds
And growing powder the plant needs . . ."

Pong-Ping's delighted. "Let's hope they
Grow well. I'll plant them straightaway!"

The two pals peer inside the box, which seems to be completely empty! "It can't be!" exclaims Pong-Ping. "There must be something inside . . ." He turns the box upside down and starts to shake it over the table. "Ah ha!" he cries as two tiny envelopes fall out, followed by a rolled up scroll of paper. "W. . .what does it mean?" asks Rupert. "Perhaps this note from my uncle will explain," says Pong-Ping as he unrolls the scroll and starts to read it carefully.

Pong-Ping smiles as he reads the note. "Uncle has sent me something to grow in the garden," he declares, and tips some seeds out of one of the envelopes. "What are they?" asks Rupert. "Chinese creeper!" says Pong-Ping. "He isn't sure how well it will grow here, so he has sent some special growing powder as well." Pong-Ping is so pleased he decides to plant the seeds immediately. "Come on!" he tells Rupert. "Let's go and choose the best spot!"

RUPERT'S PAL PLANTS SOME SEEDS

Then, with his cane, he makes a row
Of deep holes, where each seed should go.

"I wonder what the powder is?"
Thinks Rupert as they watch it fizz.

"Goodbye!" he calls. "It's time to go,
I hope your seeds soon start to grow!"

But Rupert's mother tells him how
Pong-Ping will have a long wait now . . .

Pong-Ping decides that the best place to plant the creeper is by his front porch. As Rupert looks on, he makes some holes in the ground with the end of his cane and buries each of the seeds carefully. "Now for the growing powder!" he declares. Following his uncle's instructions, Pong-Ping fills a large jug with water and stands it on the ground outside. He tips the powder into the jug and tells Rupert to stand well back. As he speaks the water starts to bubble and fizz . . .

The pals wait for the fizzing to stop, then water each of the seeds in turn. "Thanks for all your help," Pong-Ping tells Rupert. "I'll make sure you're the first to hear when they start to grow . . ." Rupert hurries home with his shopping and arrives just in time for lunch. He tells his parents about Pong-Ping's present and how his pal hopes to grow Chinese creeper all around his porch. "That *will* be nice," agrees Mrs. Bear. "But I'm afraid he'll have a long wait!"

RUPERT GETS AN URGENT NOTE

*Next morning, Rupert's father's sure
He hears a scrabbling at the door . . .*

*"It's Pong-Ping's pet!" he cries, but where
Can Pong-Ping be? He isn't there . . .*

*A note says, "Need Help – Come quickly!"
Whatever can the matter be?*

*"I'll go and see!" says Rupert. "So
will I!" his Dad says. "We'll both go!"*

Next morning, Rupert and his parents are having breakfast when they hear a strange scrabbling sound at the door. Mr. Bear opens it and is surprised to find Pong-Ping's pet dragon, but no sign of his master . . . Ming scampers towards Rupert and jumps up excitedly. "How odd," thinks Rupert. "It's not like Pong-Ping to let him out on his own." He pats Ming's head and notices a rolled-up piece of paper tucked into his collar. "Look!" he cries. "It's a note!"

Rupert takes the note and reads it out loud. "Come quickly – need help! Pong-Ping." "Oh no!" he gasps. "It sounds as if Pong-Ping's in trouble. I've got to go and help him straightaway!" "Wait a minute. I think we should *both* go and see what's wrong!" says Mr. Bear, taking a stout walking stick from the hall stand. "Do be careful!" calls Mrs. Bear as they hurry after the little dragon, off towards Pong-Ping's . . .

END OF PART 1

PART 2

RUPERT
and the Chinese Creeper

The pair set off without delay
As Pong-Ping's dragon leads the way.

They hurry forward anxiously
Then gasp, amazed at what they see . . .

"Help!" calls Pong-Ping. "The door's shut tight!
The creeper's sprouted overnight!"

"We'll get you down!" cries Mr. Bear.
"I'll fetch a ladder – just wait there . . ."

Rupert and his father have to run to keep up with the little dragon as it scampers on ahead. They catch a brief glimpse of the roof of Pong-Ping's house, but can't see any more because of the tall hedge which surrounds his garden. Making their way through a gap in the hedge, they start to hurry along a path towards the house, then stop suddenly in their tracks. "Good gracious!" exclaims Mr. Bear as he looks up and sees the extraordinary sight which lies ahead . . .

No wonder Rupert and his father rub their eyes in disbelief! The whole of Pong-Ping's house is smothered in thick, leafy creeper! "Thank goodness you've come!" calls Pong-Ping as he leans out of an upstairs window. "I woke up this morning to find everywhere so overgrown I couldn't even open the front door!" "Don't worry!" calls Mr. Bear. "We'll soon get you down!" He asks if Pong-Ping has a ladder, then goes off to look for it in the peke's garden shed.

RUPERT'S DAD TRIMS THE CREEPER

He stands the ladder up and then
Tells Pong-Ping to climb down again . . .

"I heard a strange noise," Pong-Ping cries
"Then looked outside – what a surprise!"

Then Rupert's father finds some shears.
"Exactly what we want!" he cheers.

He trims the creeper. "Now you'll see –
It just needs pruning tidily!"

Mr. Bear steadies the ladder carefully as Pong-Ping clambers down to join Rupert. None of them can believe that the creeper has grown so quickly! "I heard a strange rustling sound during the night," Pong-Ping explains. "But it was only when I drew the curtains this morning that I realised what had happened! My uncle was certainly wrong about Chinese creeper not being able to grow well in England. If it doesn't stop soon, my house will disappear!"

"I'm sure creeper doesn't grow this fast in China," says Mr. Bear. "No," says Pong-Ping and tells him about the special powder. Rupert's father nods, then hurries back to the garden shed. "A good pruning's all it needs!" he declares and emerges with a pair of shears. In no time at all he has cleared the creeper away from Pong-Ping's door and doesn't stop until there's a large heap of cuttings lying on the ground. "There!" he says. "Now let's tidy everything up . . ."

RUPERT GOES TO GET ADVICE

*The chums sweep up, Rupert says "I'll
rake all the cuttings in a pile."*

*"Look!" Pong-Ping cries. "It's back! What's more,
It's even thicker than before!"*

*What makes the Chinese Creeper grow?
"Perhaps the Professor might know?"*

*When Bodkin hears what's happened, he
gasps, "Goodness gracious! Follow me . . ."*

Rupert and Pong-Ping set to work with tools
from the garden shed and have soon gathered
all the cuttings into a neat pile. "Well done!"
says Mr. Bear. He is just about to light a bonfire
when Pong-Ping gives a startled cry. "Oh no!"
he gasps. "Look at the creeper!" Rupert turns
to look at the front of the house and stares in
astonishment. The Chinese creeper has grown
back again! "Great Scott!" cries Mr. Bear. "It
looks even thicker than it did before . . ."

Trying to prune the creeper is clearly no use.
It seems to be growing faster than ever!
Something must be done, but who can the pals
turn to for help? "What about the Professor?"
suggests Rupert. "Good idea!" agrees his father.
"Why don't you take him a cutting to examine?"
Rupert and Pong-Ping hurry to the Professor's
tower and tell Bodkin what's happened. "The
Professor's in his study," he says, "but as it's an
emergency, he won't mind being disturbed . . ."

RUPERT'S FRIEND IS PUZZLED

Their old friend can't believe his eyes.
"This plant looks very odd!" he cries.

"It's Chinese Creeper, even so
It isn't meant to grow and grow . . ."

"I don't know how to make things shrink,"
he shrugs, but Rupert starts to think . . .

"Of course!" he smiles. "I know just who
We need to show the creeper to!"

The old Professor listens carefully to Pong-Ping's story. "And this is a piece of the creeper?" he asks, peering at Rupert's cutting through a magnifying glass. He goes over to the bookcase and takes down a large book on plants. Turning its pages, he starts to compare different types of creeper until he finds one that looks just the same. "This is it!" he cries. "Look, it even says it comes from China! Nothing about it growing so large, I'm afraid . . ."

"If only we could stop the plant from spreading!" says the Professor. "Unfortunately, most people are more interested in making things grow . . ." "That's it!" cries Rupert suddenly. "Come on, Pong-Ping, there's not a moment to lose!" "Where are we going?" asks the astonished peke as they bid the Professor a hasty farewell. "To see the one group of people who don't want things to grow!" says Rupert. "I should have thought of asking them before . . ."

RUPERT VISITS THE AUTUMN ELVES

"The Autumn Elves!" he tells Pong-Ping.
"Their job's to slow down everything!"

The Elves live hidden underground,
But Rupert knows just where they're found . . .

The two pals spot a sign. "Oh dear!
We've come at the wrong time of year . . ."

"A Caretaker! I'll ring the bell,
Though he might be asleep as well!"

"But who do you mean?" asks Pong-Ping. "The Autumn Elves!" Rupert replies. "They spend a whole season making things *stop* growing in time for the winter. I'm sure they'll know what to do about the creeper . . ." Leading the way to the edge of the forest, Rupert stops in front of an old oak tree and, to Pong-Ping's surprise, pulls open a hidden door. "This way!" he tells the peke. "The Elves live underground. All we have to do is climb down these steps."

The two pals soon find themselves at the beginning of a long underground tunnel. They haven't gone far when they come to a sign which reads, 'Closed until Autumn'. "Oh dear," sighs Rupert. "I'd forgotten that the Elves all sleep during the spring!" The pair go a little further and come across a door marked, 'Caretaker – please ring'. Rupert reaches up and gives the bell-pull a sharp tug . . .

Tumbling Man

1

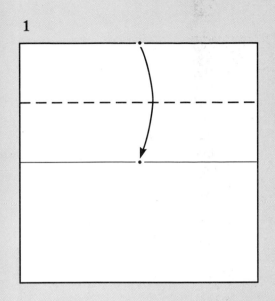

1) Fold a square of paper in half, then open out. Fold one edge to meet the centre crease.

2) Fold the opposite edge to the centre, crease and unfold.

2

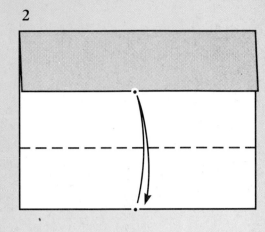

3

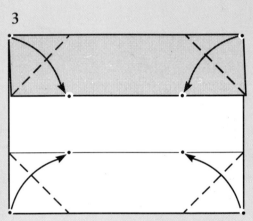

3) Fold all four corners in to meet the edge/crease (see next drawing).

4) Fold top and bottom edges in to meet the same edge/crease.

4

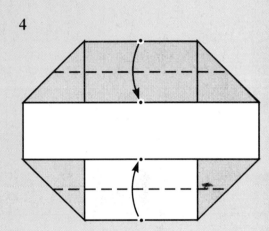

5

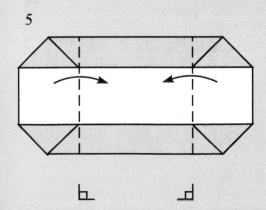

5) Fold the shorter edges to meet at the centre and open to right-angles.

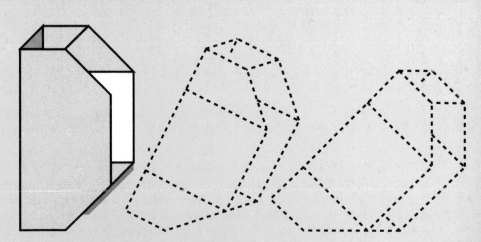

If you place the paper with the thicker edge on top, it will turn a somersault when you tip it over with a finger. Let your friends try it with the thinner end upwards – it won't work! Fold carefully and no-one will know the secret of the Tumbling Man!

Fold created by Seiro Takekawa. Supplied by Nick Robinson of The British Origami Society.

PART 3

RUPERT
and the Chinese Creeper

*A grumpy Elf appears. "You woke
me up, young bear! Is this a joke?"*

*"I'm sorry," Rupert says, "but we
Need help with something urgently . . ."*

*The Elf agrees to help the pair –
"I've just the stuff you need . . . somewhere!"*

*"This powder's guaranteed to slow
The speed at which all plants will grow!"*

At first, nothing seems to happen. Then the door swings slowly open and a sleepy-looking Elf appears, wrapped up in a long dressing-gown. "Who are you?" he asks the pals grumpily. "Don't you know we're not to be disturbed?" "S . . . sorry," stammers Rupert, "but it's an emergency! My friend's in trouble and you're the only people who can help . . ." "Dear me!" says the Elf when he hears about the creeper. "This is an unusual problem . . ."

The Elf thinks hard for a few moments, then leads the way to a large cupboard. "We once had a problem like this with some wild briars. I can't remember what we used to stop them, but it's still here . . . somewhere!" Rummaging in the cupboard, the Elf hands Rupert a small jar of cobweb cleaner. "That's no use," he mutters. "Ah ha! These are more like it!" he cries. "Growth retarder and root tonic!" Try mixing them together. They're just what you need."

RUPERT TAKES THE ELVES' POWDER

The two chums thank the little man,
Then run back as fast as they can . . .

"The creeper's grown so fast, I fear
That your house will soon disappear!"

"The only way that you and I
Can reach the plant is from the sky . . ."

The old Professor says that he
Will help the pals. "Just follow me . . ."

Thanking the Elf for all his help, Rupert and Pong-Ping hurry back along the corridor and out through the door in the tree. They run back to Pong-Ping's house as quickly as they can and are astounded to see how much the creeper has grown. "It's smothered the whole house!" cries Pong-Ping. "If we don't stop it soon, who knows what might happen!" "You're right," says Rupert. "But I'm not sure we can get near enough to sprinkle the Elves' powder."

Pong-Ping looks thoughtfully at the small jars. "Perhaps they'll work if we mix them with water?" he suggests. "Good idea!" agrees Rupert. "But how will we manage to spray the whole house?" "From the air!" declares Pong-Ping. "Let's go and ask the old Professor to lend us one of his flying machines . . ." When he hears what the pals are planning, the Professor says he's sure it's the best way to use the powder. "I've just the plane you need. Come and see . . ."

RUPERT MAKES A SPECIAL FLIGHT

"I've just the thing!" he tells the pair.
"A plane that sprays crops, from the air!"

They mix a potion up to spray,
Then fill the plane's tank straightaway . . .

"I'll fly the plane, Rupert, while you
Control the spray. Here's what to do . . ."

The plane takes off. Soon Pong-Ping sees
It disappear above the trees . . .

Leading the way to a large hangar, the Professor asks Rupert if he remembers the harvicopter. "Of course," says Rupert, "it's the plane you invented for harvesting fruit." "That's right," the Professor replies. "But it never really worked. Kept on turning everything it gathered into pulp!" He slides open the hangar door and shows the pals how he has altered the plane so that it can spray crops and trees. "Ideal for tackling your creeper!" he tells Pong-Ping.

In no time at all, the Professor and his little servant have wheeled the harvicopter out of the hangar and filled its new tank with the Elves' growth-retarding potion. "I'll need someone with me to work the spraying controls," the Professor tells Rupert. "Climb aboard and I'll show you where they are." A few minutes later, the plane starts to taxi forward, then gathers speed and takes off into the sky. "Good luck, Rupert!" calls Pong-Ping as he waves it on its way.

RUPERT STOPS THE CREEPER

Then, high above the creeper, they
Release the growth-retarding spray . . .

The creeper shrinks before their eyes . . .
"It's working!" the Professor cries.

Pong-Ping arrives, amazed to see
The creeper growing normally . . .

"I'll tell my uncle, when I write,
His creeper's reached the perfect height!"

The Professor flies up over Nutwood and circles round until Rupert can see Pong-Ping's house directly below. By now it's completely covered in creeper, which has grown right up over the roof! "Get ready to release the spray!" calls the Professor. "Five, four, three, two, one, *now*!" Rupert presses a button and is astonished to see the creeper start to change colour. "It's turning red!" he gasps. By the time they land, the creeper has already begun to shrink . . .

"Remarkable!" exclaims the Professor, "I'd never have thought such a thing was possible." The creeper carries on shrinking until, by the time Pong-Ping arrives, it is no higher than his front porch. "Perfect!" he cries delightedly. "That's just what I want." "Good," smiles the Professor. "From now on it should grow quite normally." "That's if you don't use any more of your uncle's powder!" laughs Rupert.

THE END

RUPERT and

*It's Rupert's summer holiday –
He's on his way to Rocky Bay . . .*

Each year, Rupert and his parents go to the seaside for their summer holidays. This summer they have decided to go to Rocky Bay. "I'm really looking forward to seeing the sea!" says Rupert as the train speeds along. "So am I!" smiles Mrs. Bear. "It will be lovely to hear the sound of the waves." When the train arrives, the Bears set out to look for their hotel. "It's called Sea View," says Mr. Bear.

Rosalie's Adventure

*"The hotel's name suggests that we
Should have a good view of the sea!"*

*Next morning, to the Bears' surprise,
They spot someone they recognise . . .*

At breakfast the next morning, Rupert and his parents are deciding what to do for the day, when he suddenly spots somebody he knows, walking past the window. "It's Podgy!" he cries. "He must be here on holiday too!" Rupert hurries to the front door and calls to his friend. Podgy looks all round, then gives a cry of surprise as he catches sight of Rupert. "Fancy you being here!" he laughs.

*"It's Podgy!" Rupert thinks, then he
Calls to his pal, "Hey, wait for me!"*

*"We're staying at the seaside too,
In the hotel next door to you!"*

*"That's perfect!" Rupert tells his chum,
But Podgy sighs and just looks glum!*

*"It would be, Rupert, but you see,
I'm here with Cousin Rosalie . . ."*

*"Hello!" smiles Rupert. "I hear you
Are staying for the whole week too . . ."*

Rupert is delighted to find that Podgy's holiday has just started and that his family are staying at a hotel in the same street as his own. "What fun!" he cries. "We can play on the beach together all day, build sandcastles, explore the rock-pools and see what we can catch with our fishing nets." "Yes!" agrees Podgy, but his smile suddenly fades and, to Rupert's surprise, he gives a long sigh. "W . . . what's wrong?" asks Rupert. "I thought you liked it here."

Podgy doesn't reply, but points glumly to an approaching figure dressed in a long skirt and bonnet. "Rosalie!" cries Rupert as he recognises Podgy's cousin. "Exactly!" groans Podgy. "She's staying with us all week and *I'm* meant to be looking after her!" "Coo-ee!" calls Rosalie and waves as she hurries towards the chums. "Hello, Rupert!" she cries. "How nice to see you again!" "You too," smiles Rupert. "Podgy was just saying we'll be together for a whole week . . ."

RUPERT JOINS PODGY'S PARENTS

*"That's right!" says Rosalie, but she
Complains it's boring by the sea . . .*

*"Rupert!" smiles Mr. Pig. "How grand!
We'll have a picnic on the sand."*

*The families meet on the beach.
"I've saved you all a deckchair each!"*

*"Let's build a castle!" Rupert cries.
Rosalie says she'll supervise . . .*

"A whole week at Rocky Bay!" says Rosalie. "Can you imagine anything more dull? There's hardly anything to do except walk up and down and look at the sea!" Just then, Mr. and Mrs. Pig arrive with an enormous picnic hamper. When they hear how Rupert and his parents are on holiday too, they suggest that they should all meet on the beach later that morning. "We'll set up camp!" laughs Mr. Pig. "Tell your parents I'll look out some extra deckchairs."

By the time Rupert and his parents arrive at the beach, the Pigs are already comfortably settled in their deckchairs. "Well done, Cedric!" says Mr. Bear. "This looks like an ideal spot!" Before long, Rupert and Podgy decide to go off and build a giant sand-castle. "You can come and help us if you like," Podgy tells Rosalie. "If we all work together it shouldn't take too long." "Oh, all right," says Rosalie. "But only if I can decorate it with seashells when it's finished . . ."

RUPERT BUILDS A SANDCASTLE

"I hope your castle's not too small!
You want to make it nice and tall . . ."

Then Podgy's bossy cousin tells
The chums she's off to look for shells.

"Well done!" says Mr. Bear. "Now you
Must join us for the picnic too."

They wait until Rosalie comes
Along the beach, towards the chums . . .

Rupert and Podgy start work and have soon built the main part of the castle. "It looks a bit plain!" says Rosalie. "I do hope you're going to give it some towers and windows . . ." "Of course!" says Rupert, as Podgy glowers at his cousin. "By the time we've finished, this will be the best castle on the whole beach!" After a while, Rosalie decides to go and look for some shells. "Good!" smiles Podgy. "With a bit of luck that will keep her busy all morning!"

The pals are so busy building their castle that they hardly notice the morning pass. "Bravo!" cries Mr. Bear. "You have done well!" "All that's left now is to add the shells," explains Rupert. "Rosalie went to find some ages ago, but we haven't seen her since." "I wonder where she's got to?" asks Mrs. Bear. Before Rupert can reply, a familiar-looking figure appears in the distance and comes hurrying towards them.

These two pictures of Nutwood's bonfire look identical, but there are ten differences between them. Can you spot them all? *Answers on page 93.*

PART 2

RUPERT
and Rosalie's Adventure

"I'm sorry to be late!" she smiles.
"I seemed to walk for miles and miles!"

"The castle looks delightful!" she
Tells Rupert unexpectedly . . .

Then Mr. Pig says, "Let's all play
A cricket match to end the day!"

The game begins, but Rosalie
Would rather go and see the sea . . .

"Sorry I'm so late!" puffs Rosalie. "I went further along the beach than I meant to . . ." "Never mind," says Rupert. "Come and see our castle!" "It's lovely!" cries Rosalie. "You *are* clever!" "What about the shells?" asks Podgy. "Oh, dear!" says Rosalie. "I'm afraid I had such a nice walk I forgot to collect any!" To Rupert and Podgy's amazement, Rosalie seems to have completely changed her mind about Rocky Bay. "Perfectly adorable!" she declares over lunch.

After lunch, everyone decides to play a game of cricket. "We'll form a team from each family!" says Mr. Pig. "What about Rosalie?" asks Podgy. "Which side is she going to join?" "Oh, I'd rather go for another walk!" declares Rosalie. "It's so nice by the water's edge." "If you're sure that's what you want," says Mrs. Pig. "But do try not go too far away . . ." Podgy gets ready to bat and before long the game has begun. "Have fun!" calls Rosalie as she sets off along the beach.

RUPERT HEARS STRANGE MUSIC

It's Podgy's father's turn to bat.
"We need more runs!" he cries. "Take that!"

Then Rupert is amazed to hear
Strange music playing, somewhere near . . .

"There's no-one here! It must just be
An echo of the wind and sea . . ."

Before long, Rupert starts to find
He's put the music from his mind.

Podgy and Rupert often play cricket in the summer and have soon scored more runs than anyone else. "We'll have to see about that!" laughs Mr. Pig and gives the ball a mighty swipe. "Well played, Cedric!" cries Mr. Bear as the ball flies over Rupert's head and off into the distance. Rupert hurries along the beach to get it back but as he nears the rocks where it's landed he hears a strange sound. "Music!" he gasps. "It sounds like somebody singing . . ."

Where can the strange music be coming from? Rupert looks all around, but there's no one to be seen. He tries to follow the sound, but it stops as suddenly as it started . . . "Perhaps I imagined it?" he shrugs. "Come on!" cries Podgy. "You're keeping us all waiting!" "Sorry!" calls Rupert and hurries to throw back the ball. Before long, it is Rupert's turn to bat. The game continues and in no time at all, he has forgotten all about the mysterious music . . .

RUPERT SPOTS ROSALIE

When Rosalie comes back once more
She's found some seashells by the shore . . .

"I've had a really lovely day!
I like it here at Rocky Bay . . ."

Next morning, Rupert's woken by
Bright sunshine – there's a clear, blue sky!

As Rupert gets dressed, he can see
Someone outside. "It's Rosalie!"

The cricket match ends with both teams scoring exactly the same number of runs. "Well done, everyone!" calls Mr. Pig. "Now it's time for tea!" "I'll tell Rosalie," says Rupert and hurries off to find her. "Hello," she calls. "Look at all these shells I've found to put on the castle." "They're perfect," says Rupert. "Just what we need." As soon as tea is over, Rosalie sets about arranging the shells. "What a lovely day," she smiles. "Rocky Bay's so full of surprises . . ."

Next morning, Rupert is woken early by bright sunshine streaming into his room. As he peers out of the window, he can see across the street to the hotel where Podgy's family are staying, but it's so early there's nobody about. Suddenly, the door of the hotel opens and a lone figure hurries out. "Rosalie!" gasps Rupert. "I wonder where she's going?" Pulling on the rest of his clothes, he decides to follow her and find out . . .

"I wonder what she's off to do?"
He thinks, then meets with Podgy too . . .

"Let's follow her," says Podgy, "for
She's up to something odd, I'm sure!"

She marches off, along the sand
But why? The pals don't understand!

Then suddenly, the startled pair
Can't see her – Rosalie's not there . . .

Rupert tip-toes downstairs and opens the front door. As he steps outside, he comes face to face with Podgy! "It's Rosalie!" his chum explains. "Most mornings she lies in as late as she can, but today I heard her getting ready to go out as soon as it was light! I'm sure she's up to something but I can't think what!" The pals follow Rosalie away from the town and down to the beach. To their surprise, she doesn't stop but walks briskly along the shore . . .

"Where do you suppose Rosalie's going?" whispers Podgy. "I don't know," says Rupert. "Perhaps she's decided to look for more shells." "I can't think what's come over her," declares Podgy. "When we arrived here she hated Rocky Bay, but *now* she thinks it's wonderful!" "Look!" gasps Rupert. "She's vanished!" "I don't understand," blinks Podgy. "Where's she gone?" "Come on!" calls Rupert. "Let's see what's happened . . ."

END OF PART 2

47

RUPERT
and Rosalie's Adventure

They race along the beach, but then
Hear music playing, once again . . .

"A cave!" cries Rupert. "Rosalie
Must be inside it! Follow me . . ."

"Two tunnels!" Podgy gasps. "Which way?"
Then Rupert hears the music play . . .

Next moment, to the pals' surprise,
A scene of wonder meets their eyes . . .

The pals run along the beach towards the spot where Rosalie was standing. When they get there, there is still no sign of her. "Listen!" says Podgy. "I think I can hear something . . ." "Music!" cries Rupert. "Just like yesterday, when I came here to look for the ball!" Rupert and Podgy search the beach for clues and soon find a trail of footprints leading away from the water's edge. "There's a cave here!" cries Rupert. "It must be where she's gone!"

Inside the cave, the pals discover two identical-looking tunnels. "Which way should we go?" asks Podgy. "The music seems to be coming from over here," says Rupert. "Let's try this one." The tunnel is so dark that the pair can hardly see. At last Rupert spots a pool of light glimmering ahead. "Come on," he tells Podgy. "It can't be far." The music grows louder as the chums reach the end of the tunnel. They peer into the light and gasp with surprise . . .

A cavern, where three mermaids sing
While sea creatures sit listening . . .

"King Neptune!" Rupert cries, but he
Disturbs the Ruler of the Sea!

"I'm sorry!" Rupert says. "But we
Have come to look for Rosalie . . ."

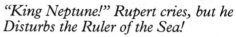

King Neptune frowns, then starts to speak,
"Has she been here? The one they seek . . ."

The tunnel opens out into a vast cavern. Seated upon some rocks around a circular pool are three beautiful mermaids, who are singing to an audience of fish and other sea creatures. Raised above them on a golden throne is a powerful, bearded figure, wearing a crown. "King Neptune!" gasps Rupert. As he speaks, the figure turns towards the pals with an angry stare. He raises his trident and the music stops. "Who dares disturb our concert?" he booms.

Everyone turns to look at Rupert and Podgy. "P . . . please, sir," stammers Podgy, "we didn't mean to interrupt the concert. We were looking for Rosalie and thought she might have come this way." "Rosalie?" asks King Neptune. "My friend's cousin," explains Rupert. "We saw her walking along the beach near the entrance to your cave . . ." King Neptune looks thoughtful, then rises to address his subjects. "Have any of you seen this land-dweller?"

*Two mermaids tell Rupert that they
Met Podgy's cousin yesterday . . .*

*Their story's interrupted by
What sounded like a far-off cry!*

*"Quick, Rupert!" Podgy calls. "Come on!
I think this must be where she's gone . . ."*

*Whatever can the matter be?
"Look!" Podgy gestures. "Out to sea . . ."*

At first nobody answers, then one of the mermaids asks Rupert what Rosalie looks like . . . "The little girl we met yesterday!" she cries. "That's right!" declares her companion. "She wandered into the cave while we were practising for the concert." "She came back later to look for some shells," adds a third mermaid. "But we haven't seen her today." "I wonder where Rosalie's got to?" asks Podgy. As he speaks, there is a distant cry from the far end of the tunnel.

The two pals race back along the tunnel until they reach the first cave. Rosalie's cries for help sound nearer, but are still quite faint. "She must have gone the other way!" cries Podgy, and hurries off to search for his cousin. Rupert follows Podgy and finds the tunnel leads to a small, secluded bay. The pair can hear Rosalie calling quite clearly now, but still can't see her anywhere. "Where can she be?" asks Rupert. "Look!" cries Podgy, pointing out to sea.

RUPERT SEES ROSALIE'S PERIL

Across the waves his cousin speeds
Inside a shell towed by two steeds!

King Neptune sees her go as well
And blows a loud note on a shell . . .

Two Tritons answer straightaway –
And swim towards the little bay.

King Neptune tells them what to do
And sends the chums on dolphins too . . .

To Rupert's amazement, he sees two white horses, galloping through the waves, towing a huge cockleshell boat. Tugging desperately at their reins is a terrified-looking Rosalie. "Stop!" she calls as the horses prance further and further away from the shore. "My chariot!" growls a low voice. The pals spin round and see that King Neptune has followed them out of the cave. "The horses must be made to stop at once!" he declares and raises a shell to his lips.

The sound of Neptune's trumpet is met with an answering call from two Tritons who come swimming towards the bay, together with a pair of dolphins. "I will do all I can to save your cousin," the King tells Podgy, "but she may need your help too." "Anything," agrees Podgy. "But what can I do?" King Neptune orders the dolphins to swim into shallow water, then tells the pals to climb on to their backs. "Hold tight!" he calls and blows his shell once more . . .

RUPERT RIDES ON A DOLPHIN

"Good luck!" calls King Neptune as they
Set off. "Don't let it get away!"

"I can't stop!" Podgy's cousin cries.
"Just hold on tight!" Rupert replies.

The horses prance and tug the reins,
"They're too strong!" Rosalie complains.

The Tritons catch the speeding pair
But Rosalie flies through the air!

At Neptune's signal, the Tritons speed off after the runaway chariot. The dolphins follow closely behind them, with Rupert and Podgy hanging on for all they're worth! As they get nearer, Rosalie recognises the chums and waves to them with her handkerchief. "Don't worry!" calls Rupert. "We'll soon get the horses to stop." "I hope so," murmurs Podgy as they start to draw level. "If you ask me, they think the whole thing's a race!"

The sea horses gallop forward, tugging the reins from Rosalie's hands. She gives a cry of alarm, but there is nothing that Rupert or Podgy can do. To their relief, the two Tritons keep pace with the runaway chariot and manage to grab hold of the trailing reins. "Hurray!" cries Podgy as the horses come to a sudden stop. Unfortunately, Rosalie is jolted backwards and loses her footing. "Oh no!" groans Rupert as she topples into the water with a loud splash . . .

RUPERT SEES ROSALIE RESCUED

Although the pals search all around
It seems she's nowhere to be found . . .

Then up she splutters, miserably,
"Come on!" says Podgy. "Ride with me!"

Now everything is calm once more
The Tritons swim towards the shore . . .

King Neptune scowls. "So you're the one
Who took my chariot for fun!"

As Rupert and Podgy urge their dolphins forward, all they can see is Rosalie's bonnet, floating on the surface of the water. To Podgy's delight, his cousin soon bobs up again, gasping for air. "Thank goodness you're all right!" he cries and hurries to her side. "But I'm not!" wails Rosalie. "I'm freezing cold, my clothes are ruined and I've swallowed gallons of water . . ." "Never mind," says Podgy. "Climb up here and we'll soon get you back to dry land . . ."

The moment Rosalie is safely aboard, the Tritons start back towards the shore, where King Neptune stands waiting. "So this is the person who dared take my chariot!" he thunders as a bedraggled Rosalie clambers ashore. "I'm sorry," she sobs. "I came to hear the Mermaids' concert, but took the wrong tunnel by mistake! When I found your chariot it seemed so splendid I just couldn't resist climbing inside . . ." "I see!" growls King Neptune.

RUPERT HURRIES BACK

Poor Rosalie's so upset he
Forgives her crime immediately . . .

"You've learned your lesson, so we'll say
No more. Now hurry on your way!"

The Pigs run back to their hotel
While Rupert goes to his as well . . .

It's clear his parents haven't seen –
For neither asks him where he's been!

King Neptune folds his arms and looks sternly at Rosalie. "I hope you've learned your lesson," he declares. "If my Tritons hadn't stopped the horses, who knows where you might have got to?" "Yes, sir," sniffs Rosalie and gives a loud sneeze. "Cheer up," smiles the King. "We'll say no more about it. Now, hurry back to your hotel and get changed before you catch a nasty cold!" "Wear this," says Podgy, draping his jacket over Rosalie's shoulders.

It is still quite early in the morning when the three companions arrive at their hotels and, to Podgy's relief, he is able to smuggle the dripping-wet Rosalie back inside without being seen. "See you later!" calls Rupert and hurries to join his parents as they settle down for breakfast. "What a beautiful day!" declares Mr. Bear. "Let's join Podgy's family down on the beach. If it stays as fine as this I think I might even be tempted to go for a swim . . ."

RUPERT AND PODGY GO SWIMMING

When everyone meets by the sea
They ask where Rosalie can be . . .

"Still sleeping!" Podgy says, "I think . . ."
And gives Rupert a secret wink!

"Hello!" says Mr. Bear. "Don't you
Want to come swimming with us too?"

But Podgy's cousin says she'll stay
On dry land for the holiday!

When Rupert and his family arrive, they find Podgy and his parents putting up a big sun-shade. "Morning, Cedric," cries Mr. Bear. "Looks like it's going to be a scorcher!" "Isn't Rosalie going to join us today?" asks Mrs. Bear. "I thought she liked the seaside." "She seems to have overslept this morning," sighs Podgy's mother. "She took ages getting ready, then came down late for breakfast." "I'm sure she'll be along soon!" says Podgy, winking at Rupert.

By the time Rosalie finally arrives, Rupert and the others are ready to go swimming. "Hello," she says. "I'm sorry to take so long but I wanted to find a good book . . ." "Aren't you going to join us for a swim?" asks Mr. Bear. "No thanks!" says Rosalie with a shudder. "I think I've seen quite enough of the sea already!" "You can say that again!" chuckles Podgy as he and Rupert hurry down to the water's edge.

THE END

RUPERT and

*"Oh, no!" groans Rupert. "Don't say I'm
Too late for breakfast! What's the time?"*

Everything is quiet in Nutwood. Another day is over and Rupert is tucked up in bed, sound asleep under a nice warm quilt. All of a sudden his alarm clock goes off with a shrill ring. "Oh, no!" he groans. "It can't be time to get up already." Throwing back the covers, Rupert clambers out of bed and draws open the curtains. "It's still dark!" he gasps as he looks outside. "It must be the middle of the night . . ."

the Sands of Time

He looks outside. "That can't be right,
It's still the middle of the night!"

His father heard the clock ring too.
"I'll come and put it right with you . . ."

Deciding that his alarm clock must have gone wrong, Rupert goes to reset it by the kitchen clock. Out on the landing he meets Mr. Bear, who has been woken by the clock's ringing and come to see what's happening. "I'll come with you," says his father. "That's odd," murmurs Mr. Bear as he looks at the kitchen clock. "It says nine o'clock, but I'm sure it was later than that when I went to bed!"

The kitchen clock's gone wrong as well –
"It should be later, I can tell!"

RUPERT'S PARENTS ARE PUZZLED

"What's happening?" asks Mrs. Bear.
"The clocks are wrong!" explain the pair.

"It's time to wake up when it's light.
Go back to bed," she says. "Sleep tight!"

Next morning, Rupert has to wait
For breakfast as the milkman's late . . .

Then Mr. Bear says, "Though I've wound
My watch up, its hands won't go round!"

By the time Rupert and his father come upstairs again, Mrs. Bear has woken up and comes to see what all the fuss is about. "How strange," she says when Rupert explains. "My kitchen clock is normally so reliable!" "I wonder what the time *really* is?" asks Rupert. "Time you went back to bed!" smiles Mrs. Bear. "I'll leave the curtains open so the sunshine will wake you in the morning. We can sort everything out after a good night's sleep."

Next morning, Rupert and his parents are woken by birds singing. "At least *they* know what time it is!" laughs Mr. Bear as he settles down to breakfast. Rupert decides to have cornflakes but finds that the milk jug is still empty. "Sorry, dear," says Mrs. Bear. "The milkman hasn't been yet. Normally he's so early!" After breakfast, Mr. Bear stares at his watch with a puzzled frown. "How odd!" he gasps. "It's ticking but the hands have stopped!"

RUPERT VISITS THE CLOCKMAKER

The milkman says he didn't wake
Because his clock made a mistake . . .

Then Rupert sees a lengthy queue
Of chums whose clocks have broken too!

The poor clock maker shuts the door.
"I just can't cope with any more!"

As Rupert wanders home he spies
An old friend. "It's the Sage!" he cries.

Mr. Bear asks Rupert to take his watch to be mended. On the way there he meets the milkman, hurrying to finish his round. "I overslept!" he tells Rupert. "Something went wrong with my alarm clock . . ." "Everyone seems to be late today," thinks Rupert. "I wonder why?" Outside the clock maker's shop, he is surprised to find a long queue of people, including his pal, Algy Pug. "Hello," says Algy. "Isn't it strange how many clocks have gone wrong?"

Rupert waits patiently outside the busy shop. It seems that everyone in Nutwood has a clock to be repaired! As Rupert reaches the door, the clock maker announces he is closing early to cope with all the extra work. "Only Father Time could mend as many clocks as this!" he declares. "I've never known anything like it . . .You'll have to come back tomorrow." On the way home Rupert spots a familiar figure striding towards Nutwood. "The Sage of Um!" he cries.

RUPERT MEETS THE SAGE OF UM

The Sage of Um's surprised to find
That Nutwood's running so behind . . .

"The Conjurer invited me
To lunch, but wasn't up, you see!"

"It's very odd!" says Rupert. "For
There's something wrong with Time, I'm sure . . ."

"In that case, Father Time must know!"
The Sage says. "Let's see where to go . . ."

The Sage of Um is a wise old man, who lives on a far-away island, together with a herd of unicorns, and travels the world in a wonderful flying umbrella. Rupert hurries to greet his friend, who asks why everyone in Nutwood seems to be so late. "Dear me!" he murmurs, as Rupert tells him all about the broken clocks. "So that explains it! The Conjurer's invited me to lunch, but when I arrived at his house they hadn't even started breakfast!"

"I wonder why everyone's clocks have gone wrong?" asks the Sage. "Perhaps Father Time might know?" suggests Rupert. "The clock maker said he was the only person who would be able to mend them all . . ." "Of course!" cries the Sage. "He's the one we need to sort things out." As Rupert looks on, his friend reaches into the pouch on his belt and produces a little book. "My travelling atlas!" he declares. "It might show us where Father Time lives . . ."

RUPERT FLIES IN THE BRELLA

He turns the pages of his book.
"That's where he must live, Rupert. Look!"

"Let's fly there!" Rupert cries, but no,
The Sage explains that he can't go . . .

"We'll hurry back to Um, then you
Can visit Father Time's home too . . .

The pair fly over Willie's house.
"Good gracious!" gasps the startled mouse!

The Sage turns the pages of his atlas to a map with an hourglass on it. "Listen to this," he says, reading aloud. "You'll find me where the hourglass stands, but first you have to cross time's sands." What does it mean?" asks Rupert. "He lives on the far side of a vast desert," explains the Sage. "Too far away for me to visit him, I'm afraid." "Can't we fly there?" asks Rupert. "We *could*," agrees his friend. "But I have to go home soon. One of the unicorns has just had a foal."

What are Rupert and the Sage to do? "I know!" cries Rupert. "If I come with you to Um Island, I can borrow the Brella and fly on to see Father Time by myself." The Sage looks doubtful, but has to admit there seems no other way of sorting out Nutwood's clocks. Unfolding the Brella, he holds it open for Rupert to climb aboard, then speaks a rhyme that sends it soaring up into the sky. "There's Willie!" cries Rupert as they fly over the roof-tops.

The Brella speeds upon its way –
"Um Island!" Rupert calls. "Hurray!"

The unicorns all come to see
Who the new visitor can be . . .

"I've told the Brella where to go
But take this compass, even so . . ."

The Sage calls out as Rupert flies
Off on his own. "Good luck!" he cries.

Leaving Nutwood far behind them, the pair fly over forests and hills until they find themselves heading out to sea towards a distant speck on the horizon. "Um Island!" cries Rupert. "That's right," smiles the Sage. "Look how the unicorns are coming to greet us . . ." The moment the Brella lands, Rupert hears a whinnying sound and sees a mother unicorn leading her little foal towards them. "Pleased to meet you," smiles Rupert, and strokes it very gently.

As soon as the Sage has fed the unicorns, he goes to his cave to get Rupert some provisions. "You'll need plenty of water," he says. "Take this compass too. You can use it to find your way if you ever get lost. Remember to make sure you're travelling in the right direction . . ." When everything is ready, the Sage sits Rupert in the Brella, then sends it on its way. "Take care!" he cries. "And good luck!"

END OF PART 1

Jester's Hat

Start with a square of paper. The colour of the facing side will form the 'face' area, the underside will make the hat itself. Fold the square in half from corner to opposite corner, crease a diagonal and unfold.

1

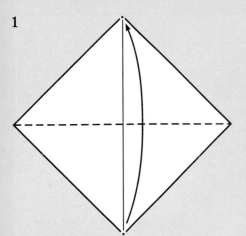

1) Fold one end of the crease to the opposite end.

2

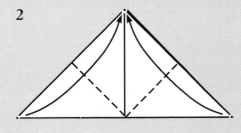

2) Take both ends of the folded edge to meet at the top corner.

3

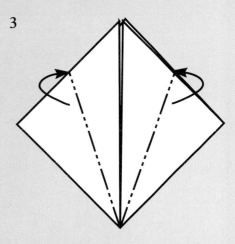

3) Fold the lower sides of the square behind to lie along the centre crease.

4

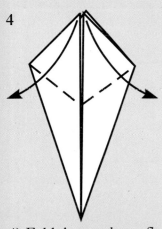

4) Fold the two loose flaps outwards to match the next diagram. The angle is not very important.

5

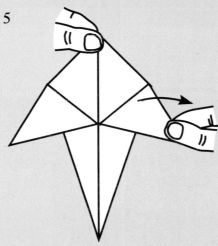

5) Holding the top corner with one hand, gently pull the right hand flap outwards . . .

6

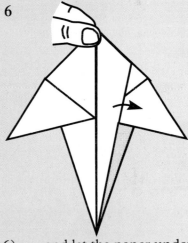

6) . . . and let the paper underneath slip out on top of it. Repeat this move on the left-hand side.

7

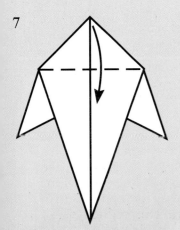

7) Fold a triangular flap downwards, creasing firmly.

8

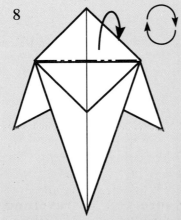

8) Take the matching flap behind and fold the tip of the triangle behind. Flatten all folds.

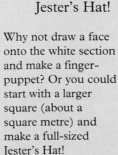

9) Turn the paper round for the finished Jester's Hat!

Why not draw a face onto the white section and make a finger-puppet? Or you could start with a larger square (about a square metre) and make a full-sized Jester's Hat!

9

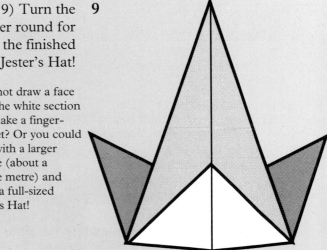

Design and method by Nick Robinson of The British Origami Society.

The Brella rises rapidly
Then carries Rupert out to sea.

He spots a great whale down below
Who seems surprised to see him go.

Then, as he flies on, Rupert sees
A distant shoreline, fringed with trees . . .

Beyond the trees he finds a land
That's empty, all except for sand . . .

As Rupert holds on tight, the Brella rises higher and higher, then spins round and speeds out to sea. Leaving Um Island behind, Rupert finds himself flying over a vast ocean, with no sign of land in any direction. He peers down and spots a little ship, but it's too far away for anyone to see. Then Rupert sees a great jet of water shoot up into the air. "It's a whale!" he cries and waves to the mighty creature, who seems to wave back by splashing the water with its tail . . .

On and on the Brella flies, until Rupert finally spots land on the horizon. "Hurray!" he cries. "I must be nearly there . . ." There are tall trees all along the shore, with thick green leaves that look very different from anything he has ever seen growing in Nutwood. He speeds over the tree-tops towards some sandy dunes which stretch far away into the distance. "This must be the start of the desert!" thinks Rupert, for all he can see is mile after mile of sand . . .

RUPERT IS CAUGHT IN A SANDSTORM

The sun beats down as Rupert drinks
Some water. "Gosh! It's hot!" he thinks.

A fierce, hot wind begins to blow –
"A sandstorm!" Rupert gasps. "Oh, no!"

Caught by the storm, Rupert finds he
Can hardly breathe or even see . . .

The Brella's buffeted about
Until, at last, he topples out!

As the Brella flies on across the desert, the sun beats down more and more intensely. "It's lucky the Sage gave me a flask full of water," thinks Rupert and raises it to his lips for a nice cool drink. All of a sudden, he hears a strange rushing sound and feels a hot wind blowing against his face. "A sandstorm!" he gasps as a huge dark cloud swirls up into the sky. With a sinking feeling, Rupert realises he is flying straight towards the storm . . .

The next moment, the sandstorm is raging all around, blotting out the light and buffeting the Brella from side to side as it carries Rupert along. The air is full of swirling grains of sands, which sting Rupert's face and force him to cover his mouth with a scarf. As the wind howls louder and louder, the Brella gives a sudden lurch to one side and Rupert loses his grip on its handle. Before he can stop himself, he is sent tumbling over the side, head over heels through the air . . .

RUPERT CRASHES IN THE DESERT

Down Rupert falls, but comes to land
Upon a large, soft pile of sand . . .

He soon stands up, relieved to find
The Brella has been left behind.

It isn't damaged, even so
He just can't seem to make it go!

"I'll have to walk!" thinks Rupert and
Sets off across the desert sand . . .

Luckily, the Brella is so full of sand that it isn't flying very high above the ground when Rupert topples out. He closes his eyes and prepares for the worst, but, to his surprise, lands with a gentle bump on a soft pile of sand. "Thank goodness for that!" he gasps as he picks himself up and watches the sandstorm disappear into the distance. Seeing that the Brella has crash-landed quite nearby, Rupert shakes the sand from his clothes and hurries over to see if it is still all right.

When he reaches the Brella, Rupert is delighted to find that it hasn't been damaged by the storm. He turns it the right way round and climbs inside. "Up and away!" he cries eagerly, but the Brella doesn't move. "Oh dear," sighs Rupert. "There must be something wrong with it after all . . ." Forced to continue the journey on foot, he folds up the Brella and takes out the Sage's compass. Lifting the Brella on to his shoulder he sets off across the sand.

RUPERT RUNS OUT OF WATER

*"A palace!" Rupert cries. "That's where
I've got to go – he must live there . . ."*

*But soon he finds, to his dismay,
The splendid building fades away . . .*

*The sun's so hot that Rupert stops
To drink, but it's the last few drops . . .*

*"I'll have to wait till later when
It's cooler, then set off again!"*

"I hope this is still the right way!" thinks Rupert. "Everywhere in the desert seems to look the same . . ." Just then he catches sight of a fabulous palace, shimmering in the distance. "That must be where Father Times lives!" he cries and hurries towards it. After a while, Rupert notices that the towers of the palace seem to be fading away . . . The next moment it suddenly vanishes altogether and he realises his mistake – it was only a mirage!

"Fancy walking all that way for nothing!" sighs Rupert. The journey has made him so thirsty he decides to have a drink of water before continuing his search. "Oh, no!" he groans as he opens the flask. "There are only a few drops left. It must have sprung a leak . . ." The sun is stronger than ever now and beats down as Rupert sets off once more. Before long, he is forced to crouch in the shade of the Brella to wait until it grows a little cooler.

RUPERT IS RESCUED

A camel train rides into view,
But is it just a mirage too?

"Stop!" Rupert calls excitedly,
And waves his scarf. "Please wait for me!"

The leading rider hears his shout
And turns the camel train about . . .

"You must be thirsty!" smiles the man.
"Drink all the water that you can!"

As Rupert shelters from the sun, he suddenly spots something moving in the distance. "It looks like a group of men on camels!" he gasps, but are they only another mirage? Springing to his feet, Rupert hurries towards the men, but soon realises that they are further away than he had thought . . . "Oh, no!" he groans. "I'll never reach them. Stop!" calls Rupert, waving his scarf in the air. "Wait!" he shouts. "Please don't go without me!"

To Rupert's relief, the camels change direction and soon the leading figure dismounts and bows in a friendly greeting. By his side stands a little boy, who smiles and says: "You must be thirsty. I will ask my father to give you a drink." The man produces a bag full of water, with a spout at one end, which he holds up for Rupert to reach. "Drink your fill," says the boy. "It is our custom to offer refreshment to strangers in need . . ."

RUPERT NEARS THE TOWER

His son says, "Join us! This is how
You can complete your journey now . . ."

They cross the sands till Rupert sees
A large oasis, ringed by trees.

"That tower's where Father Time must dwell,
Though what it's like, I cannot tell . . ."

The clock tower is surrounded by
Bright swirling stars that fill the sky.

When Rupert has finished drinking, the little boy says, "I am Yassuf. My people are nomads who travel the desert. You are welcome to join us if you wish to cross the sands . . ." "Yes, please!" smiles Rupert and is soon riding along on Yassuf's camel. "We are on our way to an oasis," declares Yassuf. As Rupert peers ahead he spots a cluster of trees, surrounded by lush vegetation. "It's just like the Sage's map!" he gasps. "I wonder if Father Time lives somewhere nearby?"

When they reach the oasis everyone gets down to let the camels drink. Rupert asks Yassuf if he has ever heard of Father Time and is told that he lives directly to the East. "I have never been there," Yassuf admits. "So I cannot tell you what to expect . . ." Thanking him for his help, Rupert takes the Brella and sets off towards a distant building. As he gets nearer he sees a giant clock tower, surrounded by swirling stars . . .

END OF PART 2

RUPERT
and the Sands of Time

Strange words are carved above the door.
"TEMPUS . . . that must mean 'time', I'm sure . . ."

The door swings open as he knocks
And Rupert hears the sound of clocks . . .

Inside, he rubs his eyes and blinks.
"There must be hundreds here!" he thinks . . .

"Hello!" calls Rupert, but finds there's
No answer. "He must be upstairs . . ."

The strange tower stands on a rocky outcrop and has a steep flight of steps leading to its only door. As Rupert climbs up them, he notices a peculiar inscription above the doorway. "Tempus fugit," he reads. "I wonder what that means?" Reaching up, Rupert raps on the heavy wooden door and is surprised to find that it swings open, all by itself . . . He steps forward to enter the building and is met by the deafening sound of hundreds of ticking clocks.

Inside the building, Rupert finds himself surrounded by clocks of every description. They line the walls of the hall-way and continue up the stairs for as far as he can see . . . "No wonder the ticking sounded so loud!" he muses. Above him swings a giant pendulum, which Rupert realises must be part of the huge clock at the top of the tower. "I wonder if that's where I'll find Father Time?" he thinks. There is no sign of anyone to ask, so Rupert decides to climb the stairs . . .

RUPERT CLIMBS TO THE TOP

*As Rupert climbs the stairs he sees
That not one of the clocks agrees . . .*

*A pendulum swings to and fro –
"Perhaps it makes the main clock go?"*

*Then Rupert stops and hesitates
He knocks upon the door and waits . . .*

*"Come in!" a voice calls, but from where?
He can't see anybody there . . .*

As he climbs the great staircase, Rupert can't resist stopping to look more closely at some of the clocks. They are all carefully numbered and, to his surprise, each one shows a completely different time! "How strange," he murmurs. "If they were all working properly, they should say the same thing . . ." Set in the walls of the stairway are circular windows, like portholes, which show glimpses of the desert outside. "I must be nearly there now," thinks Rupert . . .

At the top of the stairs, Rupert reaches a door marked "Do Not Disturb". He hesitates for a moment, then knocks firmly as he remembers the terrible muddle he has come to sort out. "Come in!" calls a loud voice. Rupert pushes open the door to reveal a cluttered room full of clocks, which look as if they are waiting to be repaired, and a huge candle burning away steadily. "This must be Father Time's workshop," thinks Rupert. "But wherever can he be?"

RUPERT MEETS FATHER TIME

Then Rupert steps inside to find
A man with clocks of every kind . . .

"I'm Father Time, but who are you?
And what do you want me to do?"

"The Sage of Um thought you might know
Why none of Nutwood's clocks will go!"

"How strange!" says Father Time. "You say
They all went wrong on the same day?"

"Don't dawdle!" calls a voice from behind the door. "Come inside and tell me what you want . . ." As Rupert steps forward, he catches sight of an old man, sitting at a workbench, surrounded by dials and cogs. "Father Time!" gasps Rupert as the old man looks up. "Correct!" snaps the old man. "Now, tell me why you've come here to disturb me at my work! I hope it's something important, little bear. Time waits for no man, you know. Not even me! I haven't got a minute to spare . . ."

"Please sir," stammers Rupert. "It's about the clocks in Nutwood. They're all broken and the Sage of Um thought *you* might be the person to put them right" "The Sage of Um?" exclaims Father Time. "If *he* sent you here, it must be serious! Sit down and tell me everything . . ." As Rupert explains how all the clocks in Nutwood went wrong on the same night, the old man strokes his beard and looks very thoughtful. "How strange," he murmurs.

RUPERT FINDS NUTWOOD'S CLOCK

He turns the pages of a book.
"Norway, Nottingham, Nutwood, look!"

"The Nutwood clock is 293.
It must be broken, come with me!"

"So that's what's wrong! I understand . . .
The window's let in lots of sand . . ."

"No wonder Nutwood's running slow!
Its regulating clock won't go . . ."

"You were quite right to come and see me," declares Father Time. "There must be something wrong with Time itself for so many clocks to suddenly stop working!" He goes over to the bookcase and pulls down a heavy ledger. "N," he murmurs, running his finger down the page. "Normandy, Norway, Nottingham . . . Ah, here it is, *Nutwood!* Clock number 293 . . ." "I don't understand," blinks Rupert. "293 is Nutwood's clock," explains Father Time.

Leading the way downstairs, Father Time shows Rupert how every clock they pass is marked with a little number. "Not much further now," he says. "There's 295 and 294, so this must be 293, the clock that sets the time in Nutwood . . ." As Rupert draws level, he sees that a porthole is wide open and grains of sand are blowing in from the desert outside. "So *that's* what's wrong!" cries Father Time. "Some sand must have got inside and jammed the works . . ."

RUPERT HELPS TO MEND THE CLOCK

*"I'll clean the works, and oil them, then
We'll soon put Nutwood right again . . ."*

*He hands Rupert a little key –
"Now you can wind it up for me . . ."*

*They clear away the pile of sand
Then put the clock back on its stand.*

*"Well done!" says Father Time. "Now we
Must launch the Brella. Follow me . . ."*

"No wonder everyone in Nutwood got in such a muddle!" laughs Father Time as he mends the clock in his workshop. "It's only my clocks that keep everyone else's running to time . . ." Do they go wrong very often?" asks Rupert. "Hardly ever!" smiles the old man. "It's my job to make sure they don't!" He cleans out the works of the broken clock and sets its hands back to the proper time. "You can wind it up," he tells Rupert, handing him a key from the ring on his belt.

Now that Nutwood's clock is working again, all that remains is for Rupert and Father Time to put it back where it belongs. "Thank goodness you came to see me," says the old man. "There are so many clocks, it might have been ages before I realised that anything was wrong!" As they finish clearing up the last of the sand, Rupert suddenly remembers the Sage's Brella. "I still don't know how to make it fly," he sighs. "Leave that to me," says Father Time.

RUPERT FLIES HOME

"Up here, it's neither night, nor day –
A rhyme will send you on your way . . ."

"Arise and journey through the skies
To where your master's island lies!"

The camel-drivers down below
Are startled to see Rupert go . . .

"Goodbye, Yassuf!" he calls then he
Speeds out across the open sea.

Rupert follows Father Time up a steep flight of steps to the very top of the tower. The sky is full of stars and the moon shines brightly, even though it is the middle of the day. "Time begins and ends here," explains the old man. "Night and day are as one . . ."Holding the Brella open, he tells Rupert to climb aboard, then speaks a strange rhyme. "Arise and journey through the skies, to where your master's island lies!" At this the Brella rises up and starts to speed away.

Leaving the clock tower far behind, the Brella skims back over the desert until Rupert spots a stand of tall trees down below. "It's the oasis!" he cries excitedly. "And there's Yassuf and his camels . . ." Rupert's friend looks up, amazed to see him flying through the air. Then he smiles and waves after the speeding Brella. Before long, Rupert has crossed the desert and reaches the coast. The Brella slows for a moment, then flies steadily out across the open sea . . .

RUPERT RETURNS TO NUTWOOD

A distant isle comes into view –
"It's Um!" he cries. "There's the Sage too . . ."

The pair set off to find out how
All Nutwood's clocks are working now . . .

"Lunchtime!" the Sage smiles happily.
"It's just as things were meant to be!"

"That must have been a quick repair;
You're back so soon!" laughs Mr. Bear.

After a while, Rupert spots a familiar-looking island and is delighted to see the Sage of Um waving from a rocky headland. "Welcome back!" he calls. "I hope Father Time was able to help you . . ." When Rupert explains how Nutwood's clock has been mended, the Sage decides to fly there at once to see how things are. "Check your father's watch," he tells Rupert as they set out in the Brella. "It's working again!" cries Rupert. "But look what time it says . . ."

"I thought so!" chuckles the Sage. "Father Time has re-set the hands of the clock so that everything in Nutwood is back exactly as it was." As he speaks, they spot Tigerlily and the Chinese Conjurer, who wave to the Sage to say he's just in time for lunch . . . When Rupert arrives home with his father's watch, Mr. Bear smiles with surprise. "Goodness," he says. "That was quick. You hardly took any time at all!"

THE END

RUPERT
and the
April Fool

John Harrold.

RUPERT'S PAL FINDS A RIDDLE

*"There's Willie Mouse! But what can he
Be looking at so carefully?"*

*As Rupert joins his pal he sees
It's slips of paper. "Look at these . . ."*

*"I saw them lying on the ground.
There's writing on each one I've found!"*

*"A riddle 'What's found everywhere
But can't be seen?' The answer's air!"*

One morning, Rupert is walking across Nutwood common when he catches sight of Willie Mouse, bending down to pick something up. "I wonder what he's found?" thinks Rupert and hurries over to join his friend. "Hello!" cries Willie. "Come and look at these. I found them all, blowing about in the wind . . ." He holds up some small slips of paper. "Perhaps it's a paper-chase?" says Rupert. "Although it's odd for someone to lay a trail without telling us anything about it . . ."

"I don't think it's a paper-chase," says Willie. "All the pieces of paper have got something written on them." "What does it says?" asks Rupert. "Each one's different," explains Willie. He hands a slip to Rupert, who slowly starts to read: " 'What is it that's everywhere around us, but nowhere to be seem?' It's a riddle!" he cries. "W . . .what's the answer?" asks Willie. "I don't know," admits Rupert, then he turns the paper over. "Of course!" he laughs. "Fresh air!"

78

"Look!" Rupert cries. "Another one!
It's like a paper-chase. What fun!"

Then Willie Mouse soon spots some more –
"The trail must lead this way, I'm sure!"

As Rupert walks along he sees
A signpost in amongst the trees . . .

"How strange!" he murmurs. "Now which way?
It doesn't really seem to say . . ."

Fascinated by Willie's find, Rupert soon spots some more slips of paper lying on the ground. "Look!" he cries. "They've all got riddles written on them . . ." "It's just like a paper-chase after all," laughs Willie. "Come on, Rupert. Let's see who can collect the most jokes." The pair start gathering all the slips they can find, then see some more, scattered among the trees by the edge of the wood. "I'm going to get those too," cries Willie, scampering on ahead.

As they set out to search for more riddles, Rupert and Willie come across a little path leading through the forect. "I've never noticed this before," says Rupert. "Let's see where it leads . . ." After a while they spot a signpost and hurry forward to see what it says. "How strange!" says Rupert. "It doesn't seem to point anywhere at all." "What does it mean?" gasps Willie. "Why would anyone put up a signpost that doesn't tell you where you're going?"

RUPERT LEADS THE WAY

*"Let's take this path!" says Rupert. "I
Feel sure that it's the best to try . . ."*

*But soon the two pals find that they
Will have to try another way.*

*"This path then!" Rupert laughs. "It's bound
To be the way. Look what I've found . . ."*

*"Another joke!" cries Willie. "Good!
The trail's unfolding as it should . . ."*

Faced with a signpost that doesn't say
anything, the two pals don't know which path to
follow next. "Let's go this way!" says Rupert.
They set off along the winding path and soon
find themselves in the heart of the forest,
surrounded by tall trees and dense vegetation.
"Where do we go now!" asks Willie. "What do
you mean?" says Rupert. "This tree's blocking
the path!" cries the little mouse. "I don't think it
goes any further. We've come to a dead end . . ."

As the path goes no further, the pals are forced
to double back until they reach the singpost once
more. "Aha!" cries Rupert. "This must be the
proper path. I can see another riddle lying on the
ground . . ." He hurries ahead to pick up the slip
of paper, then reads it out to Willie. "What time
is it when the kettle boils?" "Teatime!" laughs his
chum. "Even I know that one!" The second path
is easier to follow, and soon the pair are back in
the forest, striding out in a new direction . . .

RUPERT ENTERS A MAZE

The chums are both surprised to find
They've left the forest far behind . . .

Tall hedges meet their startled gaze –
"It's just like being in a maze!"

The pair go further on, but then
Decide they should turn back again . . .

Too late! For neither of them knows
Which way the path to Nutwood goes!

After a while, Rupert and Willie leave the forest behind them and follow the path between two tall hedges. "How strange!" thinks Rupert. "It looks as if somebody's been here and cut them into shape . . ." The next moment, they come to a gap, where the path divides yet again. "I don't see how anyone can find their way with all these twists and turns!" complains Willie. "I don't think they're meant to," says Rupert. "We seem to have wandered into some sort of giant maze!"

As the pair go on, the path gets harder and harder to follow. First it twists one way, then turns back in the other direction as if it was deliberately trying to throw them off the trail . . . "I don't like the look of this," says Willie. "Who knows where it's leading? We should turn round and start going home!" "Perhaps you're right," agrees Rupert. "It's only when the chums look back they realise they are already deep within the maze . . .

END OF PART 1

PART 2

RUPERT
and the April Fool

*"I'll lift you up, so you can see
Exactly where the path must be . . ."*

*Above the hedge, the little mouse
Can see the chimney of a house!*

*The pals decide to head for where
They see smoke rising in the air . . .*

*Inside the maze, a strange house lies
Which makes the two friends rub their eyes!*

"What are we going to do?" asks Willie. "I don't know," says Rupert. "If we could see above the hedge, getting out of the maze would be easy . . ." "We're not tall enough," says Willie. "You *will* be if I give you a leg-up!" smiles Rupert. "You're not very heavy, so it shouldn't be too hard." Soon the little mouse is peering out above the hedge. "Can you see the way?" asks Rupert hopefully. "Not exactly," cries Willie. "But I've spotted the chimney of a house."

"Well done, Willie!" cries Rupert. "I can see smoke from the chimney rising above the hedge. Let's keep walking towards it until we reach the house . . ." After a few more twists and turns, the pair suddenly come to a circular clearing at the centre of the maze. "Look!" gasps Willie. "That must be the house, but isn't it odd!" "I'll say!" agrees Rupert, "look at the way the chimney curls round . . ." "And the curtains," cries Willie, "they're all on the outside!"

"How strange!" says Rupert. "No front door!
But there's a bell-pull here, I'm sure . . ."

He rings the bell and straightaway
The flowers drench Willie with their spray!

"There is a front door, after all –
It's just been painted like the wall!"

Inside the house, strange mirrors shrink
And stretch the pals – "How odd!" they think.

Although the house looks so strange, Rupert and Willie decide to ask whoever lives there how to get out of the maze. "I'll just ring the door-bell," says Rupert, then suddenly notices that there isn't any door! "That *looks* like a bell pull," says Willie. "Let's try it anyway and see what happens . . ." As Rupert tugs the handle, all the flowers in the window box swivel round and squirt poor Willie with water. "Tricked!" he splutters. "It must happen to everyone . . ."

As Willie shakes himself dry, the two pals hear the creak of a door swinging open. "It was here all the time!" gasps Rupert. "But somebody's painted it to look just like part of the wall!" Venturing inside, the pair find themselves in a hallway full of tall mirrors . . ."Look at my reflection!" laughs Willie. "It's just like a fun-fair!" Rupert peers into the glass and sees that his reflection looks funny, too. "Everything in the house seems to be a joke," he murmurs.

RUPERT CLIMBS THE STAIRS

*Rupert calls out. "It seems that there's
Nobody here, let's try upstairs . . ."*

*The pair climb up the stairs, but then
Find that they're going down again!*

*"Another joke!" laughs Rupert. "Keep
On climbing – now they're getting steep . . ."*

*They reach a landing lined with books,
But is it everything it looks?*

"Hello!" calls Rupert. "Is anybody there?" No one answers, and the chums begin to think that the house must be empty after all. "Let's try looking upstairs," suggests Rupert. "There's nothing down here except the hall of mirrors . . ." As they climb the staircase, Willie notices that all the pictures are hanging upside down. "Another joke!" laughs Rupert. But as he speaks, he stumbles on the stairs. "I don't believe it!" he gasps. "We've started to go back down again . . ."

"These stairs are as bad as the maze!" puffs Willie. "First they go up, then they go down, and now they're even steeper than ever!" "Never mind," says Rupert, giving his chum a hand. "We can't have much further to climb, I think I can see the top from here . . .' The pair reach a landing lined with tall, cluttered bookcases. "At least *they* look fairly normal," says Willie, still recovering his breath. "Yes," agrees Rupert. "But look at the window. It's completely upside down!"

RUPERT MEETS THE JESTER

"Joke books!" cries Rupert. "Let me see,
I wonder which the best will be?"

The bookcase moves, then Rupert hears
A cry as Willie disappears!

"A secret door!" It opens wide
And Rupert joins his pal inside . . .

"Well done!" a voice calls. "You're my guests!
I hope you both enjoyed my jests . . ."

Looking at the bookcases more closely, Rupert and Willie discover that all the books are about jokes and riddles. "There must be hundreds!" gasps Rupert. "I wonder what they're like?" says Willie and reaches out to take one down. The moment he touches the shelf, he gives a cry of alarm, for the whole bookcase suddenly starts to move! "Look out!" calls Rupert, but it's too late. Before he can do anything, the bookcase swings right round, and Willie disappears . . .

"A secret door!" gasps Rupert. He pushes on the bookcase with all his might, but nothing happens. He tries again and this time there's a loud click. "Come in!" cries a cheerful voice as the bookcase swings round. "You've done well to find me. Not many people manage to get through the maze!" At the far end of the room sits a little man, dressed in a jester's outfit. "I'm so glad you've come," he says. "You're just in time to hear my latest riddle!"

RUPERT'S PAL SAVES THE DAY

*"I write the riddles that appear
In Christmas crackers every year!"*

*"I lost a brand-new batch when they
Caught in the wind and blew away . . ."*

*"The jokes we found!" cries Willie, then
Hands all the riddles back again . . .*

*"That's wonderful! Hip, Hip, Hurray!
I think I'll take a holiday!"*

"What sort of bulb do you keep indoors?" "A hyacinth?" suggest Rupert. "No! A light bulb, of course!" chuckles the little man. "Jokes are my business. I write them all year round, to go inside Christmas crackers!" "That must be fun!" says Willie. "Sometimes," agrees the Jester, "but it's jolly hard work! Imagine having to think up a new set of jokes every year . . ." "This year's even busier than normal," he sighs. "I'd just finished a batch, when they all blew out of the window . . ."

"You don't mean these, do you?" asks Willie, pulling a bundle of slips from his pocket. "Rupert and I found them lying on the ground as we made our way through the maze . . ." "Why did the chicken stay where it was? What pair of coins can you ride? That's it!" cries the Jester. "You've gathered up all the riddles I lost. Now I won't have to try and think of them again . . . My work's nearly done for the year! Hip, hip, hurray! This calls for a day off, to celebrate!"

RUPERT IS TRICKED

"We need to get to Nutwood now,"
Says Rupert. "Can you show us how?"

The Jester smiles. "Not straightaway!
I thought you'd like to stay and play . . ."

"I know!" he cries. "I'll hide somewhere
And you can come and find me there!"

"Good luck!" calls out the little man.
"Now, come and catch me, if you can!"

"I'm glad we were able to help you," says Rupert. "If you're having a day off, perhaps you could show Willie and me the way back through the maze?" "Back?" cries the Jester. "But you can't go yet – you've only just arrived. There's plenty of time to reach Nutwood . . ." he laughs. "Before you go, I thought you might like to play a game. What shall we start with? Charades? Pass the Parcel? Blind Man's Buff? I *like* games nearly as much as making up jokes!"

"I know!" cries the Jester. "Let's have a game of Hide and Seek!" Jumping from his swing, he runs towards a shiny metal pole, which goes down through a hole in the floor. "I'll hide and *you* can look for me!" he laughs. "Come back!" calls Rupert, realising that without the Jester's help they won't be able to find their way home. "Too late!" groans Willie as the Jester slides out of sight. "Catch me if you can!" he chuckles.

RUPERT
and the April Fool

"Come on!" calls Rupert. "Don't delay!
We mustn't let him get away . . ."

Wherever will the Jester hide?
"It looks as if he's gone outside!"

"The maze!" calls Rupert. "Follow me!
I should have guessed that's where he'd be . . ."

Inside the maze the two chums hear
The Jester call, "You're getting near!"

"We mustn't let him get away!" says Rupert. "Let's slide down the pole as well." "Us?" gasps Willie. "I . . . I'm not sure I can!" "Come on!" cries Rupert. Taking a firm grip, he glides down through the hole in the floor and finds himself back in the hall of mirrors. "It's easy!" he calls up to Willie. Taking a deep breath, the little mouse shuts his eyes and slides slowly down the pole. "Look!" cries Rupert. "The front door's wide open. The Jester must have gone outside . . ."

The pals can see no sign of the Jester, but are sure they can hear him laughing behind the tall walls of the maze. "Come on!" calls Rupert. "He can't be far away." Inside the maze, the path is as confusing and difficult to follow as ever. "Which way should we go?" asks Willie. "I don't know," says Rupert. Just then a voice calls out, "You're getting warm, you're getting near, but still can't find me, that's quite clear!" "The Jester!" cries Rupert.

RUPERT'S PLAN WORKS

Then Rupert knows just what to do,
"We'll ask the Jester riddles too!"

The Jester answers, "Ask me more . . ."
"He's that way!" Rupert says. "I'm sure . . ."

"Keep cracking jokes!" he tells his chum.
"I'll go to where the answers come . . ."

The Jester falls for Rupert's plan –
He creeps towards the little man . . .

Although the Jester is somewhere near, Rupert and Willie soon realise it's almost impossible to find him in the middle of the maze. "His voice is our only clue," says Rupert, then he smiles as he has a sudden idea . . . "I say!" he calls. "What sort of tree never gets cold?" "A fir tree!" cries the Jester. "Which is the most athletic vegetable?" "A runner bean!" the Jester exclaims. "It's working," Rupert whispers. "He can't resist a joke! It sounds as if he's over here."

"So far, so good!" Rupert tells Willie. "You stay here and call out some more jokes, while I try to find exactly where the Jester is hiding . . ." "I say, I say," cries Willie, as Rupert tip-toes away, "What sort of cakes are thinner than all the others?" "That's easy!" laughs the Jester. "Pancakes, of course! Ask me another . . ." As he speaks, Rupert finally catches sight of him, hiding behind a tall hedge. "If only Willie can keep him talking for a little longer," he murmurs.

RUPERT WINS THE GAME

The Jester's taken unawares –
"We've beaten you!" Rupert declares.

"Well played!" the Jester smiles. "You won!
But goodness me, our game was fun!"

"Hello!" he calls to Willie. "You
Did well to think up new jokes too . . ."

He shows the chums the way to go –
"I'll miss you, when you've gone, you know!"

"I, um, I can't remember any more jokes!" stammers Willie from behind the hedge. "Then it's my turn to ask you," laughs the Jester. "When is a . . ." he breaks off with a startled cry as Rupert jumps up and grabs him by the arm. "Caught you at last!" he declares. "You won't get away so easily *this* time . . ." To Rupert's surprise, the Jester doesn't seem to mind losing at all. "Well played!" he chuckles. "That's the best game of Hide and Seek I can remember!"

Now that Rupert and Willie have won the game of Hide and Seek, the Jester agrees to show them the way back to Nutwood. "Are you sure you haven't got time for just one more?" he asks eagerly. "No," says Rupert. "We really must be getting home for tea!" As the pals follow the twists and turns of the path, the Jester gives a heavy sigh and shakes his head sadly. "Not many people manage to find my house," he declares. "It's rather lonely, living in a maze . . ."

RUPERT MAKES A NEW FRIEND

"Perhaps we'll come another day,"
Says Rupert. "All my friends could play . . ."

"Or come to Nutwood for, you see,
Tomorrow it's my birthday tea . . ."

Next day, the party's in full swing
When Willie hears the doorbell ring . . .

The Jester's late – "I got lost too,
In the maze, on the way to you!"

"It would be fun to play more games," agrees Rupert. "Perhaps some of my chums from Nutwood could join in too . . ." "I know!" cries Willie. "It's my birthday tomorrow, and I've invited everyone to a party. Why don't you come as well?" "Really?" asks the Jester. "Of course!" smiles Willie as they reach the edge of the common. "Perhaps you could tell a few jokes." "I'd be delighted!" beams the little man, bidding the chums farewell as they hurry on their way.

The next day, Rupert joins all his chums at Willie's party. When they hear about the maze the two pals have discovered, everyone is keen to know more about the Jester and his extraordinary house. "You'll be able to meet him soon!" laughs Willie. "He's promised to come and join us this afternoon." Just then, the doorbell rings and Willie hurries off to open the door. "Hello!" smiles the Jester. "Sorry I'm late, but I took a wrong turn on my way through the maze!"

RUPERT ENJOYS WILLIE'S PARTY

The chums ask their new friend if he
Will tell some riddles after tea . . .

"Of course!" he laughs. "They're all brand-new,
I'd like to try them out on you!"

The party ends and everyone
Agrees that it has been great fun.

The two pals wave goodbye and then
The Jester sets off home again . . .

In no time at all the pals are sitting down to a splendid party spread. "This *is* fun!" cries the Jester. "I can't remember meeting so many new friends!" As soon as tea is over, Willie asks him to read out some jokes. "I'd be delighted!" he smiles. "What's so friendly it spends all its time waving?" "The sea?" suggests Gregory. "A fan!" laughs Tigerlily. "What goes up but never comes down?" Nobody can guess, so the Jester has to tell them. "Smoke, of course!" he chuckles . . .

At the end of a fun-filled afternoon, all the chums say goodbye to Willie and set off home across the common. "Thank you for asking me to your party!" exclaims the Jester. "It was even better than our game of hide and seek!" "I wonder if we'll see him again?" asks Willie, as he and Rupert wave goodbye to their new friend. "I hope so," says Rupert. "But I'm not sure we'd ever find our way back through the maze . . ."

THE
END

92

Follow Rupert every day

in the Daily Express

John Harrold.

ANSWERS TO PUZZLE:
Spot the Difference: (page 43) 1. Algy's bow-tie missing; 2. Podgy missing; 3. Windows missing church tower; 4. Feather missing guy's hat; 5. Pocket missing Mr. Bear's jacket; 6. Rung missing ladder; 7. Tree missing (right-hand corner); 8. Door missing house (right-hand corner); 9. Chin-strap missing Growler's helmet; 10. Patch missing guy's trousers.

ORIGAMI:
If you have enjoyed the origami pages, you can find out more about the British Origami Society by writing to its secretary, Pete Ford, at the following address:
British Origami Society,
11 Yarningdale Road,
Kings Heath,
Birmingham B14 6LT.

John Harrold.